Lighthouse Mouse™ Meets Simon the Cat

(A Cat and Mouse Tale)

Susan Anderson Coons
Illustrated by Don Sanne

Order this book online at www.trafford.com
or email orders@trafford.com

Most Trafford titles are also available at major online book retailers.

The Lighthouse Mouse. =Independnent Publisher's IPPY Bronze Award. Ibakon Gretl and the
Stinky, Sticky Dragon, 2010, Harnessing Motion, This Fresh Pursuit, Wine Song,
The Chariots Have Left the Heavens, KHUM radio show Rendezvous.

Printed in the United States of America.

ISBN: 978-1-4669-1223-6 (sc)
ISBN: 978-1-4669-1224-3 (e)

Trafford rev. 05/16/2012

 www.trafford.com

North America & International
toll-free: 1 888 232 4444 (USA & Canada)
phone: 250 383 6864 ♦ fax: 812 355 4082

Dedication to: Daphne Jordan, Christie Scannell, Dean Warner, Margaret Coons, Sharon Bacchus, Shelly Ledfords, Judy Cheung & Mary Rudge of California Federation of Chapparel Poets and Artist Embassy International, Jerry Silva, LeRoy Hawkins, Karen Dorsey, Edith Richmond who critiqued this work.

One stormy day, Lighthouse Mouse and Molly, the lighthouse keeper's daughter, cleaned windows. Winds outside howled like unwanted guests. Bushes shook like complaining pests.

Racing downstairs with Mouse in her pocket, Molly slipped and stumbled. Hitting her shoulder while mouse tumbled in her backpack, Molly cried, "Ow!!! Ouch!! With my pinched shoulder and your sore back, you and Simon the Cat can stay on the couch when I'm at school. Then I won't worry about you."

Mouse was not certain about playing with cats. They might raise the hair on their back and hiss a mean hiss! Mouse shook his head and said, "Thank you, Molly. You are kind, but I must say, 'No . . . About this I do mind!'"

Molly patted Lighthouse Mouse and rubbed her sore shoulder. "I must go to school and leave you two together. Treat each other like you want to be treated. That's called, 'The Golden Rule'. When I return and you two are playing in harmony so sweet, I'll bring you a treat."

Simon meowed in protest as Mouse shook his head and squeaked, "I spent all summer on this couch while you were home. Now that you are in school doesn't mean that I must follow this thing called 'The Golden Rule'. This makes me feel like a grouch. It's a disgrace for a respectable Mouse to be replaced by a Cat on this couch. Think of that!"

As if to answer, Simon pounced up on the couch. Not knowing what Simon wanted, Mouse dove between cushions. Simon meowed his answer. It made Mouse shiver. "I'll send you back to town . . . or have you for lunch," Cat said.

Mouse twitched his whiskers up, then down.

Winds rattled windows. "EEEEE. OOOOO. SHHEE. SH.. SHOO." Hinges shook. Doors creaked. The lighthouse sounded so scary that Mouse remembered what it was like to be alone. Simon the Cat must know about that, too.

Molly whispered. Reminding them, "I need you both as friends. Help me with this." As she talked, slowly, their tempers and furs settled down.

Just then, the clock chimed eight times as Molly added, "I'm late for school! Let's work this out when I get home. Until then, be good!"

In tears, Simon the Cat added, "Molly, I've been The Big Cheese here for years! Lighthouse Mouse slips into our house and you want me to applaud?"

Mouse twitched his whiskers, stomped and pranced on paws.

"I'll shoo you away, Cat, if you come near this couch! I'll squeak and creek and keep you awake at night. Even your sleep will get no pause."

As if to answer Lighthouse Mouse, Simon stared, and stared and stared.

Mouse studied Simon's the Cat's big, mean stare. "What can I do??" Mouse wondered. Then, he remembered earlier times when he had asked the Great One to keep him safe from the gales. The Great One had sent Molly. Great One would keep Mouse safe—even from Simon's cold, hard stare.

"Teach us how to be friends," Mouse asked The Great One. "When we learn, Molly will treat us like her brothers."

As he prayed, Mouse worried. " If Simon the Cat pounces on me, my stay in the cottage might end. I might be his lunch."

Boldly, Mouse prayed again. "Days are long when Molly is gone. Winds and waves are scary. Help us, Great One, to care for each other. You can even show Cat a bit more about that."

Then Mouse squeaked to Simon, "Winds outside sound like thunder. Together, we'll be brave and not have to wonder. Won't you like that, Mr. Cat?"

The more Mouse squeaked, the more he knew. They could ignore Grumpy Old Cat and Mouse tales about chasing and fighting. "Hooray, for a new kind of friendship and play!" Mouse boldly told Simon.

Looking down at Simon, Mouse whispered, "Cat, let's chat. We can do puzzles and help Molly. With her sore shoulder, she needs us to make things right." The more that Simon frowned, the more that Mouse got the picture. They both cared for Molly,..but . . . making friends with each other that might be too much!

Then . . . Mouse thought of Molly and how much she needed them. Changing his mind, he told Simon . . . "Why not? Tales that we can't like each other were told by a Grump without a brother. I'll teach you to jig. You teach me to whisker twitch and pounce on light!"

"We won't worry about wild, windy sounds," Mouse said. "We'll be helpers at the Lighthouse until Molly comes home. She'll be so glad that we remembered 'The Golden Rule' that she'll laugh and play and heal faster. We'll call ourselves 'The Lighthouse Keepers'and have a better world than if we played alone."

Simon added up his choices as he mumbled, "Being a bully is easy. Any cat can do that. On one paw, no respectable cat plays with a mouse. On the other paw, . . . having a friend might be better than hearing winds howl . . . alone."

Mouse chuckled as Simon added, "Hmm . . . Mouse, You might not be such a pest, after all."

Quickly, Mouse stuck out his paw and said, Let's shake and see what a difference we can make. We can do it! "

Mouse watched Simon nod his head and then sent up more prayers.

"I'll have to flee, unless we can be freed from Old Cat and Mouse Tales . . . . Besides, if we help Molly, she will be more jolly."

"Look," Mouse argued. When Molly is at school, there is little to make us smile," Mouse said. "We can wander hills—mile after mile, but there's nothing inside to do, except wait for Molly for a long while—or roll marbles by ourselves."

Mouse added, "Marbles are more fun with two than one."

"We'll help Molly sweep the hall . . . Her shoulder will heal faster. We'll tell cat tales, a few mouse and human ones about life before we became a band of three."

Simon added up his choices one more time. On the one paw, no respectable cat plays with a mouse . . . On the other paw . . . being a friend might be better than hearing winds howl . . . alone. I won't know if I don't give it a try. Then Simon told Mouse again, "Mouse, You might not be such a pest, after all. Let's be friends."

Mouse stuck out his paw and said, "Let's shake and see what a difference we can make!"

Mouse climbing down from the sofa, Mouse danced as he heard Simon announce, "Let's be the official, Lighthouse Cat and Mouse Team instead of two fighting . . . cat and mouse critters. Visitors might wonder when we help each other, but Molly will know she has two very kind . . . brothers.

Simon the cat grinned his best grin and agreed. "Sounds good to me. We'll help Molly from day into night."

Just then they heard steps on the porch. A key turned. "Creek, creek." As Molly opened the door, even the hinges squeaked a happy squeak.

Molly looked at them on the floor with shoulders together and smiled. "I wondered about you when I left for school, but I didn't want to tell one of you to go outside with the other one cozy by the fire. When I leave you here now, you can sing and play and not be stuck in separate corners like grouches.

Proudly, Simon invited Mouse, "Come, ride on my back. Think about that! A mouse and cat friendship has such a nice ring. We'll sing at weddings and birthdays like kings. Wonder of wonders! Friendships are better than fighting or thundering. No shoving, or shoving . . . or pushing. We'll be friends from the couch to the ground."

How they danced! They pranced! They skipped to the idea of how cats and mice can be nice to each other all day long.

Such a new kind of song!

Every day, they helped Molly clean up crumbs. They swished dishes, straightened pillows—polished windows. "Bumble, crumble, swish, glish. Sprinkle, skip and whisker twitch," they sang in their new friendship cheer.

As Mouse had promised, in the cottage together they worked puzzles, sang songs and no longer worried about wild and windy sounds outside. They were "Keepers of the Lighthouse" until Molly came home. She was so glad that they remembered that "Golden Rule" idea and it was a better world than if they had played alone.

Then one windy day, a storm outside howled—even harder than ever. Rattling fiercely, it blew open the lighthouse door beyond their cottage. "Simon! Look!" Mouse shouted over the roaring winds. "Let's get over there and fix that door!" Running down the path, they leaned against the shaking door, but it would not close.

Lighthouse Mouse gave his loudest squeak! Simon the Cat howled! They spotted Molly racing across the field from the cottage towards them. Puffing and panting, she reached them and leaned across the outside of the door with them.

With all three pushing against the door, the rattling door still did not close shut. Desperate, Molly shouted to her Mom and Dad upstairs in the lighthouse. "Dad! Mom! Help! The wind is blowing us away from here!"

Bracing themselves against the door, Molly, Lighthouse Mouse, and Simon the Car pushed harder.

Panting and pushing, Molly grabbed a chair and the three new friends braced the chair under the door handle to hold it as Molly's Mom and Dad came running down the stairs of the lighthouse.

With Molly's parents beside them, Simon, Mouse and Molly calmed down. As the door held firm and closed with one last complaining rattle, they all breathed a sigh of relief.

"Wow! Meow!" Cat shouted.

"We did it! Squeeeel! Wheee!" Agreed Mouse as the others added their victory cheers.

How they celebrated! They danced! They pranced at the very idea that a cat and a mouse with the help of human friends could do things that they could not do alone.

Inside of the lighthouse, Lighthouse Mouse, Simon the Cat, helped as Molly and her Mom and Dad put the lighthouse back in order. They cleaned tools, polished windows, cleaned broken limbs on the path.

"Bumble, crumble, swish and glish. Springle, skip and whisker twitch," they all sang with a happy cheer as Simon the Cat and Lighthouse Mouse did a happy jig for all of them.

Lighthouse Mouse chuckled as he thought of all that had happened. Even that Golden Rule thing seemed easier to understand as Molly explained that it meant treating each other like they wanted to be treated.

"Humpty, Dumpty, Dumpity, Lum," they sang. "Having no friends is not as much fun. Friends are good with two and better with three. "Humpty, Dumpty, Dumpity, Wheee!"

As they finished their song, Lighthouse Mouse added, "When we're a team, we make better music than when we sang those Grumpy Old Cat and Mouse Songs."

How they all chuckled when Molly, Mom Dad, Lighthouse Mouse and Simon the Cat thought of what had happened and how they had conquered those fierce storms. To celebrate Mouse and Simon gave each other a big hug of appreciation and everyone breathed a big sigh of relief. There would be peace in that lighthouse they knew.

At that moment, Lighthouse Mouse whispered shyly, "Let's give thanks to The Great One for helping us learn how to get along. We are having more fun now than when we were alone. After all, I did ask."

Joining hands the lighthouse team, agreed and sang,

"Humpty, Dumpty, Dumpity Lum. Having a friend is the best fun of all."

"HUMPTY DUMPTY. DUMPITY, LUM... HAVING NO FRIEND IS NOT FUN AT ALL.

"FIDDLE DEE DEE!. FIDDLE DEE DOO! "A FRIEND IS GOOD WITH TWO, BUT BETTER WITH THREE.

When the storm was over, Molly, Lighthouse Mouse and Simon the Cat went out to sit on the hill to watch the sunset--as cozy as only good friends and family can be. "Humpity, Dumpity, Dumpity, Lum. Working together is much more fun. Humpty, Dumpty, We have a new tune. Friends are good with two and better with three.

The End.

Printed in the United States
By Bookmasters